DAILY LIFE

The Underground Railroad

P.M. Boekhoff and Stuart A. Kallen

KIDHAVEN PRESS

An imprint of Thomson Gale, a part of The Thomson Corporation

THOMSON

GALE

Detroit • New York • San Francisco • San Diego • New Haven, Conn.
Waterville, Maine • London • Munich

© 2005 Thomson Gale, a part of The Thomson Corporation.

Thomson and Star Logo are trademarks and Gale and Kidhaven Press are registered trademarks used herein under license.

For more information, contact
Kidhaven Press
27500 Drake Rd.
Farmington Hills, MI 48331-3535
Or you can visit our Internet site at http://www.gale.com

LIBRARY OF CONGRESS CATALOGING-IN-PUBLICATION DATA

Boekhoff, P. M. (Patti Marlene), 1957–
   The Underground Railroad / by P. M. Boekhoff & Stuart A. Kallen.
   p. cm. — (Daily life)
Summary: Discusses the daily life of slaves escaping the south using the Underground Railroad. Includes information about escape routes, code words, quilt codes, and the people who operated the network. Includes bibliographical references and index.
   ISBN 0-7377-2607-5 (alk. paper)
1. Slaves—United States—Biography—Juvenile literature. 2. Slavery—United States—History—Juvenile literature. 3. Underground Railroad—History—Juvenile literature. [1. Slaves. 2. Slavery. 3. Underground Railroad]
   I. Title. II. Series.

Printed in the United States of America

Contents

CHAPTER ONE

Slavery and Escape

Slavery is the act of forcing one person to work for another without pay. It is an ancient practice. Six thousand years ago, people were used as slaves in the land now known as Iraq. Slaves also built the pyramids in Egypt. And slave traders sold Africans as slaves to European settlers in America for hundreds of years. James L. Bradley, an African man enslaved in America, explained how he was captured and sold into slavery:

> I think I was between two and three years old when the soul-destroyers tore me from my mother's arms, somewhere in Africa, far back from the sea. They carried me a long distance to a ship; all the way back I looked back, and cried. The ship was full of men and women loaded in chains; but I was so small, they let me run about on deck. After many long days, they brought us into Charleston, South Carolina. A slaveholder bought me. . . . He sold me to a Mr. Bradley, by whose name I have ever since been called.[1]

Under slavery, people were bought and sold for money by those who claimed to own them. Slaves could be beaten, whipped, or tortured by the people who claimed to own them. This treatment was used to break their spirits so they would not run away. Former American slave Solomon Northrup talked about the heartbreaking experience of a young slave girl who was whipped:

> The painful cries and shrieks of the tortured Patsey, mingling with the loud and angry curses of Epps, loaded the air. She was [stripped of skin]. . . . We laid her on some boards in the hut, where she remained a long time, with eyes closed and groaning in agony. . . . A blessed thing

The great cities of ancient times were built by slaves. Here, slaves move a statue into an ancient Egyptian city.

it would have been for her . . . had she never lifted up her head in life again. [T]he sprightly, laughter-loving spirit of her youth [was] gone. She fell into a mournful and [disheartened] mood, and oftentimes would start up in her sleep, and with raised hands, plead for mercy. She became more silent. . . . A care-worn, pitiful expression settled on her face. . . . If ever there was a broken heart . . . it was Patsey's.[2]

Slavery in the South

Such treatment kept many enslaved people too afraid to dream of freedom. By the end of the 1700s about 1.5 million people from Africa worked as slaves in the United States. They made up about half of the population in southern states such as North Carolina, South Carolina, Georgia, Mississippi, and Alabama. Many of these people were used to work on large farms, called **plantations**, where crops such as cotton, sugar, and tobacco were grown.

The largest plantations in the Deep South might use up to five hundred people as slaves. Men were used to cut down trees, dig ditches, drive wagons, and care for the farm animals and crops. Others worked as carpenters, brick and stone masons, furniture makers, cobblers, blacksmiths, and barbers.

Some women were used to cook, sew, clean, nurse the sick, care for animals, and raise crops. Older women cared for slave owners' children and slave children too young to work. They also spun wool and cotton into yarn and made it into clothing. Others made items such as soap, candles, beer, and bread.

In addition to working on plantations, slaves worked at other tasks. They mined gold, dug for coal, made iron, and worked on fishing boats. Slaves built thousands of miles of roads, canals, and railroads. They worked on docks or in factories where cotton and tobacco were processed. They also worked in hotels, bars, and restaurants. They were sailors, soldiers, mechanics, tailors, firemen, and more.

By the end of the 1700s one and a half million slaves, almost half the population of the Deep South, worked on plantations.

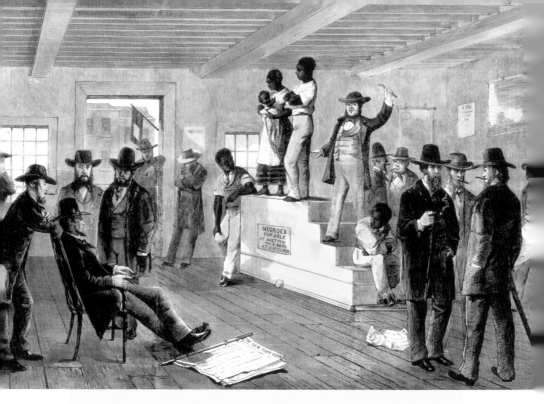

Slave families were often torn apart as individual members were sold at auctions to different buyers.

Together and Apart

A slave's life was often one of toil and misery. Big plantations in the South were known for the worst cruelties to slaves. On those plantations many people were chained up at night and worked to death. Slaves had many reasons to run away, but the main reason was to stay with loved ones who were about to be sold to a far-away plantation.

Slave owners tore families apart, selling husbands, wives, and children to different buyers. Family members were not allowed to cry or show emotion when their mothers, fathers, sisters, and brothers were taken away. If they did, they might be beaten or whipped.

Frederick Douglass, an escaped slave who became a great leader, said, "The whip we can bear without a murmer, compared to the idea of separation. Oh, my friends, you cannot feel the slave's misery when he is separated from his kindred. The agony of the mother when parting from her children cannot be told. There is nothing we so much dread as to be sold farther south."[3]

Some slaves decided to run away because they had been beaten and abused. Others simply wanted their freedom. They would rather risk death as a runaway than live as a slave. They did not believe that human beings should be owned by other human beings. They wanted to think for themselves and make their own decisions.

A Place to Run

Slave owners separated families and people who knew each other to make it more difficult for them to think for themselves and plan an escape together. They passed laws against teaching slaves to read and write, and made them have a permission slip to go on errands without a slave owner. They did all they could to keep the slaves ignorant, scared, and alone, with no safe place to go.

There were a number of places a runaway slave could go, however. Some ran away into the woods where they hid in caves or built hidden shelters. Others built homes and raised their families in swamps and thick woodlands. Often these places were not far from the plantations where their friends and relatives were still held in slavery. Runaway slaves often helped their enslaved neighbors and visited them in secret, offering help to those trying to escape.

Runaways who needed a place to hide could move from one secret shelter to the next. Sometimes they were helped by Native Americans, who knew all the hidden places in the wilderness. Some tribes, such as the Seminoles of Florida, took runaways into their families and married them. And some European settlers who did not believe in slavery also helped the runaways.

Between 1780 and 1830 northern states gradually outlawed slavery. They became free states, where people who were able to escape from slavery could live in freedom, instead of in hiding. But even in the free states, slave hunters could capture runaways and bring them back to slave states. And it was against the law for anyone to help them escape, so many former slaves ran farther north into Canada, where the laws protected them from slave hunters.

A Legend

By the 1820s a growing number of slaves were running away from farms and plantations in the South. In 1826 a slave named Tice Davis escaped across the Ohio River from the slave state of Kentucky to the free state of Ohio. Although his owner followed him across the river, Davis seemed to disappear on the other side of the river.

The puzzled slave master combed the countryside but could not find Davis. He later said Davis must have escaped on an "underground road." The rumor of the

After being sold to another owner, a slave anguishes at being taken away from her family.

Slave hunters were rewarded for returning runaway slaves to their owners.

slave who escaped on the underground road changed as it was told over and over and became legend. By this time, trains were the fastest new way to travel, and storytellers began to say that Davis had escaped on an "underground railroad."

Although it usually was not always underground, and it was not a railroad, by the 1830s there was a system of secret routes and safe houses where slaves could hide on their journey from the South all the way to Canada. People along the way opened their homes and businesses to runaways, creating **stations** on the railroad line. They built a secret **network** of friends that became known as the Underground Railroad.

CHAPTER TWO

Secret Friends

While a train rarely carried slaves to freedom, railroad words were used to disguise the illegal activities of the Underground Railroad. Escaped slaves were called passengers. Those who led runaways on the safest routes through forests and farmlands, across swamps and rivers, were called **conductors**. They drove carriages, rowed boats, and hid people on ships and trains.

Conductors led passengers to safe houses called depots or stations. Some of these were connected with underground tunnels to barns or other depots. If slave hunters arrived, the passengers could escape through these tunnels.

People who lived in depots were called stationmasters. Stationmasters provided food, clothing, tools, shelter, hiding places, information, and travel directions to passengers on the Underground Railroad.

Secret languages were a very important part of the Underground Railroad. Former slave Ambrose Headon explained, "We always called 'freedom' 'possum,' so as to keep the white people from knowing what we were talking about. We all understood it."[4]

The Grapevine

The **routes** of the Underground Railroad were most often developed by black people who were able to travel and discover the best ways for others to make their way north. Some were free blacks who had been granted freedom by their owners. Others worked at extra jobs to earn enough money to buy their freedom and even buy their families from slave owners. A few had fought in wars and were given freedom for their service.

Fugitive slave families arrive at an Indiana farm. The farm is a busy station of the Underground Railroad.

Slaves who traveled worked secretly with free blacks to pass along information about escape routes. For example, slaves who were hired out to work in towns exchanged information and remembered routes between places. Slaves who worked as sailors relayed messages between people in the North and people in the South, and arranged for escapes on the ships they worked on.

Enslaved blacks traveling as drivers or servants were able to meet secretly with free blacks at the plantation owners' favorite inns. Free blacks formed their own neighborhoods in big cities like New Orleans and Charleston. They sheltered runaway slaves and helped them find work through the Underground Railroad network.

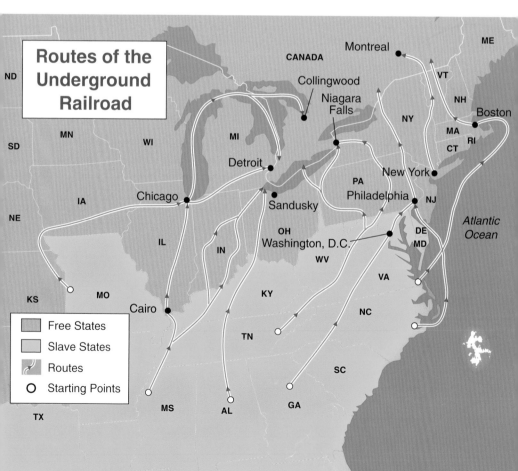

People who helped runaways learned about other people who could be trusted to offer food, shelter, and work, and they built a secret network of friends and friends of friends. By the 1840s the loosely organized Underground Railroad was helping thousands of people to escape slavery every year.

Spirited Away

Churches and temples were very important stations on the Underground Railroad. Worshippers provided shelter, clothing, and food and gathered information for successful escapes. Some worshippers secretly taught slaves to spell and read the Bible.

The Society of Friends, also known as the Quakers, was among the first white religious groups to work on the Underground Railroad. They publicly called for slavery to be ended, or abolished, and were known as **abolitionists**. They banned slavery among their followers and set an example for others with their bravery and kindness.

But the Quakers were not completely free from the prejudice of the times. "They will give us good advice," wrote former slave Samuel Ringgold Ward. "They will aid in giving us a partial education—but never in a Quaker school, beside their own children. Whatever they do for us savors of pity, and is done at arm's length."[5]

One of the first underground churches, the First African Baptist Church, was organized in 1775 on a plantation. In the 1800s its members built a church in Savannah, Georgia. It had a tunnel under it that connected to the many underground passageways below

Underground Code Words

Code words were used to disguise the activities of the Underground Railroad. Here are some examples:

Code Word	Meaning
Baggage	Escaping slaves
Bundles of Wood	Slaves to be expected
Conductor	A person who led slaves along escape routes
Drinking Gourd	The Big Dipper and the North Star
Forwarding	Taking slaves from station to station
Load of Potatoes	Slaves hidden under produce in a wagon
Passengers	Escaping slaves
Parcel	Slave to be expected
Preachers	Leaders of the Underground Railroad
Station	A safe house
Stationmaster	Keeper of a safe house
Stockholder	A person who donated money, food, or clothes

the city. Runaways hid from slave hunters under the floor of the church, which had diamond-shaped holes in it to provide fresh air.

Underground Music Codes

Worshippers at churches such as the First African Baptist sang gospel songs, also called sorrow songs. Sometimes these songs had double meanings that contained secret messages about the Underground Railroad. For example, if people were singing songs about a sweet chariot or a gospel train, it might mean there was an escape happening in the neighborhood that people might join in. The song might give clues about times and places.

Sometimes people stomped on the floor and clapped their hands. These loud rhythms were used to cover up

Slaves got together to sing songs about the Underground Railroad. These songs contained secret messages about escaping on the Underground Railroad.

the sounds of people escaping. And sometimes the rhythms themselves carried a secret meaning. In Africa, people used the rhythms of drums to communicate in **codes** between villages and tribes who spoke different languages. For this reason, drums were not allowed on plantations, but people communicated with rhythms in other ways.

Dancers tapped out rhythms with their feet and clapped out rhythms with their hands. Blacksmiths wheezed out rhythms on their **bellows** that were echoed in songs sung across the plantation. The rhythms and the words carried secret messages about when to escape, and how, and where.

Songs with double meanings, musical communication, and the rhythms of talking drums were forms of communication understood by many slaves. Together, these formed part of the secret language of the Underground Railroad.

Underground Quilt Code

Secret messages were passed in other ways, too. One of the few reasons enslaved men and women were allowed to be together was to make quilts. The people created a secret language in the patterns in the quilts, based on ancient African art that carried hidden meanings. The person who was teaching the secret codes appeared to be simply teaching quilting patterns, and would be praised for helping the slaves learn new skills.

It was very common to hang quilts out over a fence to air out during the day. So the quilts with their secret language could be hung out one at a time for all to see

Underground Quilt Codes

Slaves and members of the Underground Railroad used patterns in quilts to pass messages. Here are some examples:

 The **Monkey Wrench** quilt square told slaves to prepare the tools they would need to escape.

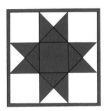 The **North Star** quilt pattern reminded slaves to follow the North Star, and it would help lead them out of the south.

 The **Bear Paw** instructed slaves to follow bear tracks to find food and water.

 The **Flying Geese** quilt square provided slaves with navigational direction.

without raising any suspicions among slave owners. The slaves used the patterns in the quilts to direct escapes. The quilts could be read as maps, with the squares representing farms or plantations. The stitches showed rivers, hills, and other landscape features. The knots counted out the distances between safe places to hide.

Quilts were used as signals all along the escape routes north. One sign of a safe house was a quilt with a Log Cabin pattern hanging outside. Another was the Jacob's Ladder quilt pattern, a **sign** of an Underground Railroad station where people were ready to help.

Secret Helpers

Quilts made by escaped slaves were given as gifts to stationmasters, who used them as a railroad station sign. For example, Harriet Tubman escaped from slavery in 1849 and walked to a house on the Underground Railroad. She gave the woman there the only thing she owned, a quilt.

After gaining her freedom, Tubman decided to help others escape. For the next fifteen years, she went back to the South nineteen times to lead about three hundred people out of bondage. "I never run my train off the track and I never lost a passenger,"[6] said the famous conductor.

Tubman carried a pistol to protect her passengers and convince frightened passengers not to turn back. She also carried medicine to put crying babies to sleep. Tubman had a great sense for when danger was near, and she sang gospel songs that told her passengers when to hide and when to come out.

Passengers on the Underground Railroad faced danger, fear, pain, and hunger. But many strangers

After escaping from slavery, Harriet Tubman helped about three hundred slaves make their way north on the Underground Railroad.

were secretly friends. The many invisible helping hands of the Underground Railroad often made the difference between freedom and death on the dangerous journey out of slavery.

CHAPTER THREE

Life on the Run

Although the Underground Railroad provided a way to escape, runaways faced great danger. Those who were captured on the run were severely punished. Some were burned at the stake or tortured as a lesson to the others. Captured runaways could have a foot broken or cut off or receive hundreds of lashes from a bullwhip. Some were branded on the face with a hot iron so if they escaped again, other slave owners would know that they were runaways.

The Best Time to Run

Runaway slaves had much to lose. It was very important for them to know when to run so they would have the best chance of finding freedom. Conductor William Still wrote: "Slaves sometimes, when wanting to get away, would make their owners believe that they were very happy and contented. And, in using this kind of foolishness, would keep up appearances until an opportunity offered for an escape."[7]

The best time to escape was usually Saturday night, while the owners went out to parties. The next day,

Sunday, when the other slaves were in church, a runaway was less likely to be missed.

Running away on Saturday night was good for another reason. When slaves were discovered missing, slave owners often placed ads in newspapers or printed fliers offering large rewards for their return. No fliers or newspapers were printed on Sunday, so there could be no notices posted until Monday, giving the runaways a head start.

Dangerous Animals

Because of the danger of being spotted and captured during the day, most runaways hid during the day and ran during the night. They had to stay away from the main roads, traveling hundreds of miles. They hid in

Runaways who were caught and returned to their owners were severely punished.

Frederick Douglass was an escaped slave who became one of the greatest leaders of the abolition movement.

forests, fields, and swamps and on mountains. There were many dangerous animals in these places, including bears, alligators, scorpions, snakes, and wild boars.

Abolitionist leader and former slave Frederick Douglass said he often wondered whether slavery would be better than the doubts and fears of escaping. When planning his escape, he thought about the dangers:

At every gate through which we had to pass, we saw a watchman; at every ferry, a guard; on every bridge, a sentinel, and in every wood, a patrol or slave-hunter. We were hemmed in on every side ... upon either side, we saw grim death assuming a variety of horrid shapes. Now, it was starvation. ... Now, we were hunted by dogs, and overtaken and torn to pieces by their merciless fangs. We were stung by scorpions—chased by wild beasts—bitten by snakes. ... No man can tell the intense agony which is felt by the slave, when wavering on the point of making an escape.[8]

Bloodhounds

The most dangerous animals for the runaway slave were the bloodhound dogs that slave hunters used to chase them. A bloodhound could smell a piece of clothing worn by the runaway slave, and it could follow the scent of that person for miles through the woods. If the bloodhounds caught up with a runaway, the dogs might rip him or her apart with their teeth.

To prevent this, many slaves made friends with the plantation dogs, fed them and played with them. Runaway James Smith was followed by a friendly plantation

Bloodhounds could follow the scent of a runaway slave for miles.

dog, which ripped out the throat of an attacking bloodhound and sent the others off in fright. Another runaway gave her last crumbs of food to attacking bloodhounds. The dogs licked her hands and ran off into the woods to play.

Passengers on the Underground Railroad also learned how to throw off the bloodhounds' scent. Some runaways brought along raw onions or pine sap to rub on their shoes or bare feet. Crossing over a body of water, jumping in a creek, or walking in a swamp also washed away the smell of footprints. When slaves heard the plantation owners preparing to unleash the bloodhounds, they gave warning to nearby runaways by loudly singing: "Wade in the water children, Wade in the water, God's gonna trouble the water."

Freedom River

Waterways were very important routes of the Underground Railroad. A song called "Follow the Drinking Gourd" directed the escaped slaves to follow the little rivers to the big river while keeping their eyes on the Drinking Gourd.

The Drinking Gourd is a nickname for a pattern of stars now known as the Big Dipper, which includes the North Star. Runaway David Holmes explained,

Heard about that from an old man, a slave, who had gone off a good many times; but he never had the luck to get right away. He used to point out the North Star to me, and tell me that if any man followed that, it would bring him into the

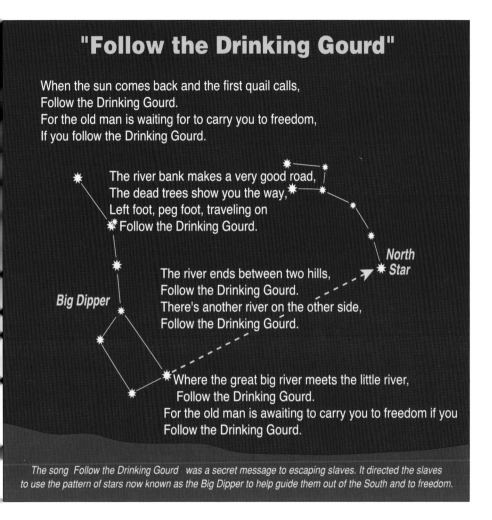

"Follow the Drinking Gourd"

When the sun comes back and the first quail calls,
Follow the Drinking Gourd.
For the old man is waiting for to carry you to freedom,
If you follow the Drinking Gourd.

The river bank makes a very good road,
The dead trees show you the way,
Left foot, peg foot, traveling on
Follow the Drinking Gourd.

The river ends between two hills,
Follow the Drinking Gourd.
There's another river on the other side,
Follow the Drinking Gourd.

Big Dipper

North Star

Where the great big river meets the little river,
Follow the Drinking Gourd.
For the old man is awaiting to carry you to freedom if you
Follow the Drinking Gourd.

The song Follow the Drinking Gourd was a secret message to escaping slaves. It directed the slaves to use the pattern of stars now known as the Big Dipper to help guide them out of the South and to freedom.

north country, where the people were free; and that if a slave could get there he would be free.[9]

Following the Drinking Gourd north along little rivers led to the big river. The big river was the Ohio River, which divided the free state of Ohio from the slave state of Kentucky. The Ohio River is long, wide, and deep, and the water moves fast. Only a few places were safe to take passengers across by boat. Slave hunters and bloodhounds gathered along the big river at these crossings.

Over the River

Underground Railroad conductors used signals and secret signs to direct the escapes across the Ohio River at night. For example, a call like a hoot owl was a signal of nearby conductors with a boat. A free black man pretending to rave drunken nonsense by the river might actually be giving coded instructions for escape. At one crossing, people walking along the shore softly

The cupola on top of this safe house, still standing in Illinois, may have been used to signal fugitives.

tapping rocks together signaled passengers to come out of hiding in the woods so they could row them across the river and lead them to an Underground Railroad station.

There were many secret places and signs to watch for on the Underground Railroad. Houses and barns near the river sometimes had tunnels to the water. This provided an underground road from the river to the Underground Railroad station. Safe houses had signs such as a lamp glowing in a window, a flag in the hand of a lawn statue, or a row of bricks painted white on the chimney.

Passengers also used secret signs to ask to come in. They might call out with the voice of a whippoorwill bird or knock softly three times on the station door. Often, when someone inside asked "Who is there?" the correct answer was "A friend with friends." If the right signal was given, the door opened and the passengers stepped on board the northern line of the Under-ground Railroad.

CHAPTER FOUR

The Northern Line

Although slavery was banned in the northern states, it was illegal for northerners to help people escape slavery. In the North as well as the South, those who took part in the Underground Railroad put themselves in danger to help others gain freedom. Some workers were caught and went to jail for years. Others were given fines so large that they lost everything they owned trying to pay them. Sometimes slave owners set fire to Underground Railroad depots and even killed conductors and station-masters. Free blacks who worked on the network could be captured and sold into slavery themselves.

Many stories about the Underground Railroad are lost because of these dangers. Books against slavery were banned in the South, and in the North angry mobs smashed printing presses and sometimes killed abolitionist newspaper editors. John Mason wrote about his experiences escaping from slavery, being cap-tured and sold back into slavery, and escaping again. He later rescued more than two thousand slaves.

Friends with Friends

One hundred steps led from the northern shore of the Ohio River up to the home of Reverend John Rankin in Ripley, Ohio. Rankin was a friend of John P. Parker, an author who lived in Poke Patch, Ripley's African American community. Almost every night when the river was not frozen, Parker rowed over to Kentucky, where he had once been a slave.

When no slave catchers were lurking, Rankin lit a lantern in a high window in his house on the hill. Guided by the lantern, Parker and other conductors brought people across the river in the dark of night.

Though slavery was banned in northern states, when captured, slaves were returned to southern states and sold back into slavery.

Reverend John Rankin hung a lantern in the high window of his home on the Ohio River to let runaway slaves know they would be safe in his house.

Rankin and his friends waited on the bottom step to pull runaways up to safety.

Like many conductors on the Underground Railroad, Parker led a double life. By day he calmly went about his business. But at night he risked his life to help more than one thousand people escape to freedom. In Kentucky there was a wanted poster offering one thousand dollars for Parker's capture, dead or alive. Slave catchers tried to catch him, and spies watched him. They sent fake runaways to lure him into traps, but Parker and his wife and friends uncovered the plots.

At the Stations

One night, daring Underground Railroad workers freed some runaways from slave catchers who were bringing them to jail, then back south into slavery. The slave catchers brought an armed crowd to Parker's house to search for them. Parker fooled them by saying loudly they could search the whole house, even the roof. The passengers hiding in the attic knew that Parker was secretly telling them to move up to the roof.

But they were still not safe, so Parker led the passengers to his cabinetmaker friend Tom Collins, who also made coffins. Collins hid Parker and the passengers in unfinished coffins. The slave catchers searched his shop, looking into all the cabinets, but they did not care to look into the coffins on that gloomy night. No one thought

Runaway slaves who were captured could be beaten, tortured, branded with a hot iron, or even burned at the stake.

that people who were running for their lives would want to hide in coffins. Everyone escaped.

The President and the First Lady

Parker knew another worker on the northern line named Levi Coffin, a Quaker who housed about three thousand runaways and became known as president of the Underground Railroad. Among his many deeds, Coffin founded the Free Labor Movement to prove that slavery was not needed to make a profit. The movement organized farms, factories, and stores to make and sell cotton and other goods without the use of slave labor.

Coffin's wife Kate organized a sewing circle of women who collected and mended blankets and warm clothing for passengers. Such circles of friends collected money, medicine, food, shoes, and other items. They also made rag dolls to comfort runaway children on their journey through the night.

Sometimes Coffin's sewing circle made disguises for passengers who were surrounded by slave hunters. In one such escape, Levi Coffin wrote,

> The males were disguised as females, and the females as males, . . . seated in elegant carriages, and driven out of the city at different points, exactly at noon, when most people were at dinner. Those who were on the look-out for a company of frightened, poorly-dressed fugitives, did not recognize the objects of their search, for it was quite common for the colored gentry to go out riding in that style.[10]

The Fast Train

Some daring passengers traveled by day on boats or trains. Sewing circles made beards and padded clothing and collected hats and other disguises for them. But the disguised passengers had to be ready to jump off a train or boat at a moment's notice if their secret was discovered.

Some passengers who traveled openly were given legal papers that said they were free blacks. These were used as passports. Some were false papers, and some belonged to people who were dead or safe in Canada. In Baltimore two women, one black, one white, were

After the Civil War, many former slaves went north on the same rivers the runaways had used when escaping on the Underground Railroad.

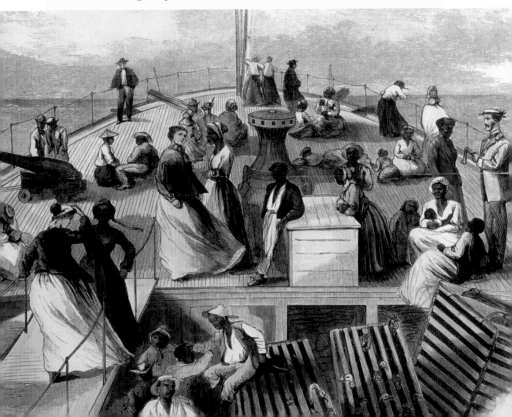

among the Underground Railroad workers who collected the papers so they could be passed from one passenger to the next.

Although there were a few spectacular daring escapes in the open, most passengers stayed hidden. Many rode with conductors in carriages in the middle of the night. Sometimes they rode in secret compartments in wagons under loads of vegetables or hay. Often conductors gave them directions to walk ten to twenty miles to the next station.

Canada

With the help of brave conductors, thousands of runaways crossed the border into Canada. Many worked as blacksmiths, carpenters, or farmers to earn the money to buy their own farms. The weather was cold, but the land was inexpensive and could be paid for in installments. People built homes, businesses, schools, and communities. Some were able to buy family members out of slavery or help them escape to Canada as well.

Most of the newcomers were young men who were more skilled than the poor local laborers. Former slave Susan Boggs said, "If it was not for the . . . law, we would be mobbed here, and we couldn't stay in this house. The prejudice is a great deal worse here than it is in the States. The colored people can always get more money than the laboring white people, because they can do the work better."[11]

The End of Slavery

In 1861 the Civil War began in the United States. Armies of the North fought those in the South in a war to end

When the Civil War ended, African Americans who fought for the North were discharged from the Union army.

slavery. More than 185,000 black soldiers fought for the North, and nearly one-fourth of them died. Harriet Tubman and others led raids to free slaves. As the South was destroyed by the war, more people than ever escaped slavery. After the war ended in 1865, slavery was abolished forever in the United States and the slaves were soon set free.

African American speakers, artists, writers, and inventors continued the struggle to improve the lives of all people. Harriet Tubman and many others worked for the rights of women and helped start black schools. All across the South, whole families who were finally allowed to read and write went to school together.

While enslaved, carpenter Ambrose Headon was sent to build a college. In 1878 he wrote:

> While at work on this college, I fell into a conversation with the white carpenters at work there, and they said "niggers" would do nothing "if set free". I told them if they would take me out into the woods and strip every rag from me, and set me free, that in ten years I would school my children. . . . [N]ow all my children are good scholars; one is a minister; one has charge of an academy; I have a good house of seven rooms, and eleven acres of land about it, besides a farm of 320 acres in the country. Nothing can illustrate the great change that has come over us, unless it is the change in passing from earth to heaven.[12]

Notes

Chapter One: Slavery and Escape

1. Quoted in John W. Blassingame, ed., *Slave Testimony: Two Centuries of Letters, Speeches, Interviews, and Autobiographies.* Baton Rouge: Louisiana State University Press, 1977, p. 687.

2. Quoted in John F. Bayliss, *Black Slave Narratives: Life Under Slavery as Told by Its Victims in America.* New York: Macmillan, 1970, pp. 89–90.

3. Frederick Douglass, *Frederick Douglass in His Own Words.* San Diego, CA: Harcourt Brace, 1995, p. 10.

Chapter Two: Secret Friends

4. Quoted in Blassingame, *Slave Testimony,* pp. 744–45.

5. Quoted in Benjamin Quarles, *Black Abolitionists.* New York: Oxford University Press, 1969, p. 72.

6. Quoted in Charles L. Blockson, *The Underground Railroad: Dramatic Firsthand Accounts of Daring Escapes to Freedom.* New York: Berkley Books, 1987, p. 86.

Chapter Three: Life on the Run

7. William Still, *The Underground Railroad.* Chicago: Johnson, 1970, p. 212.

8. Frederick Douglass, *My Bondage and My Freedom.* New York: Arno, 1968, pp. 282–84.

9. Quoted in Blassingame, *Slave Testimony,* p. 298.

Chapter Four: The Northern Line

10. Levi Coffin, *Reminiscences of Levi Coffin.* New York: Arno and *New York Times,* 1968, p. 315.

11. Quoted in Blassingame, *Slave Testimony,* p. 420.

12. Quoted in Blassingame, *Slave Testimony,* p. 745.

Glossary

abolitionist: A person who acted to abolish, or do away with, slavery.

bellows: A windbag that pumps air onto a fire to make it burn hotter.

code: A system of words or symbols with double meanings used for secret messages.

conductor: A person who is in charge of a railroad train. Also a person who led runaways on the safest routes along the Underground Railroad.

network: A group of people who have similar interests and stay in contact and help each other.

plantation: A large farm on which people live and raise one main crop.

route: A road or way to travel from one place to another.

sign: An act, motion, sound, or material thing that stands for an idea, information, or plan.

station: A stopping place for taking on passengers along a route.

For Further Exploration

Raymond Bial, *The Underground Railroad*. Boston: Houghton Mifflin, 1995. With words and pictures, this book describes the lives of the passengers and the conductors of the Underground Railroad, and the stations they traveled through on their way to freedom.

Ann Heinrichs, *We the People: The Underground Railroad*. Minneapolis, MN: Compass Point Books, 2001. Key events in the history of the Underground Railroad.

Sally Senzell Isaacs, *Picture the Past: Life on the Underground Railroad*. Chicago: Heinemann Library, 2002. This book tells what life was like for escaping slaves and how people helped them along the way.

Ellen Levine, . . . *If You Traveled on the Underground Railroad*. New York: Scholastic, 1988. This book looks at what it would be like to be a former slave escaping on the Underground Railroad.

R. Conrad Stein, *Cornerstones of Freedom: The Underground Railroad*. New York: Childrens Press, 1997. Describes the stations and conductors of the Underground Railroad and how the network worked to help slaves escape in the United States before the Civil War.

Index

Picture Credits

Cover image: © The Bridgeman Art Library
AP/Wide World Photos, 30
© Bettmann/CORBIS, 15
© HIP/Scala/Art Resource, NY, 5
© Layne Kennedy/CORBIS, 34
© North Wind Picture Archives, 11, 12, 19, 23, 25, 26, 27, 33, 35, 37, 39
© Scala/Art Resource, NY, 7

About the Authors

P.M. Boekhoff is an author of more than twenty-five non-fiction books for children. She has written about history, science, and the lives of creative people. Boekhoff is also an artist who has created murals and theatrical scenic paintings and has illustrated many book covers. In her spare time she paints, draws, writes poetry, and studies herbal medicine.

Stuart A. Kallen is the author of more than 160 non-fiction books for children and young adults. He has written on topics ranging from the theory of relativity to the history of rock and roll. In addition, Kallen has written award-winning children's videos and television scripts. In his spare time he is a singer/songwriter/guitarist in San Diego, California.

DATE			